THE RAGE OF THE SEA WITCH

Roland Chambers lives on a small tumble-down
farm on Dartmoor with his family and other
livestock – a dog, a cat, some pigs and chickens,
and occasionally, wandering hill ponies.

THE ADVENTURES
OF BILLY SHAMAN

THE RAGE
OF THE
SEA WITCH

ROLAND CHAMBERS

ZEPHYR

An imprint of Head of Zeus

This is a Zephyr book, first published in the UK in 2023
by Head of Zeus Ltd, part of Bloomsbury Plc

Text and illustrations copyright © Roland Chambers, 2023

9 7 5 3 1 2 4 6 8

A catalogue record for this book is available from the
British Library.

ISBN (PBO): 9781789541465
ISBN (E): 9781789541441

Designed by Jessie Price

Printed and bound in Great Britain by
CPI Group (UK) Ltd, Croydon CR0 4YY

For Susan, Nelly, Benjy and Sam

1

I want to tell you the story of Billy Shaman, because if I don't tell it, nobody else will. As to why I think it's so important, or who I am, you shall find out shortly. Let's not be in a hurry. Let's just start at the beginning, in a strange house, where Billy's parents (very selfish people) were about to abandon him for the summer holidays, with nothing to do but wander its many rooms and walk in the garden.

'See if you can find the source of that river,' said his mum, pointing to a stream. 'Draw a map.'

'Look at these orchids, Billy,' said his dad, reaching into his pocket for a magnifying glass. Billy's mum was a famous explorer. His dad was interested in flowers and bugs. Each had a nickname for the other. His dad was Rusty, because of his bright red hair. His mum was Spider, because of the ropes she used to scale mountains and to swing down into canyons. It made them sound exciting and special, but Billy was plain Billy, because he'd never done anything much at all. At school, the closest he'd come to having a nickname was 'Billy S', because there were three Billys in his class.

'You can't seriously be leaving me here for the whole holidays?' grumbled Billy, knowing perfectly well that was exactly what was going to happen.

His parents ignored him.

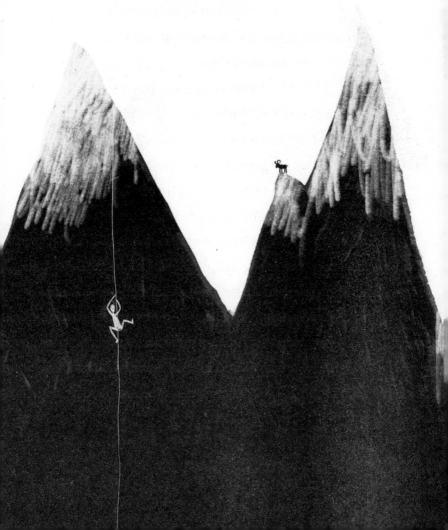

'See this one here?' said his dad, kneeling in the grass. 'That's a little marsh orchid.'

His face was tender.

'As soon as you've gone,' Billy muttered, 'I'm going to stamp on it.'

He wasn't surprised his parents were leaving him alone. Every summer was the same, though the house was always different. Some had dungeons. Others had greenhouses.

Last year he'd stayed in an empty castle owned by a famous mountaineer. This year it was a sort of museum owned by a group of people interested in science, or flowers, or something. He'd already forgotten. He didn't care. His parents weren't even going on holiday with each other. His dad was flying to South America, his mum to Africa. Meanwhile, Billy was staying in the strange house on his own, with only the caretakers to talk to – Mrs Cript and her husband, Mr Cript, who looked like a gargoyle.

'I hate orchids,' he said bitterly.

'Nonsense,' said his dad, putting his hand on Billy's shoulder. 'I know you don't mean it.'

'I do,' said Billy. 'I hate orchids and I hate you.'

'Oh, Billy,' said his mum.

'Don't be difficult,' said his dad.

'It's not as if we're deserting you,' said his mum, looking at her watch.

'Not at all,' agreed his dad,
opening the car door so that Billy's
mum could climb in.

Mr Cript, the gargoyle, was driving
Billy's parents to the station.

'Think of it as a wonderful present,'
continued his dad. 'This house to explore. This
garden. The whole summer ahead of you!' He
sighed. 'What I wouldn't give to be a boy of
your age.'

'Come on, Rusty,' said Billy's mum.

'All right, Spider.'

Billy watched until the car vanished round
a corner of the long drive and even the growl
of the engine disappeared. He looked at
the orchid at his feet, but he didn't feel like
stamping on it any more. He could hear a bird
singing, but he didn't know what sort of bird
it was.

'Well, come in if you're coming,'
said a voice, and when he turned,
there was Mrs Cript. She didn't sound very
encouraging. She looked as though she didn't
care what he did, as long as she was not
expected to do it for him.

So he picked up his suitcase and followed
her inside.

2

That evening, Mrs Cript explained the rules of the house.

'You're welcome to explore,' she said, 'but don't touch any of the exhibits. Don't run or shout in the corridors, or disturb Mr Cript when he's working in the garden.'

She spoke with a Scottish accent.

'These things are *forbidden*,' she said, 'but do make yourself at home. Supper is at six. Breakfast is at eight.' She leaned forward. 'Eight o'clock precisely.'

Billy's bedroom was in the attic and smelled of mould. To make things worse, it was haunted. That first night, he couldn't sleep because of a breathing sound. There was no mistaking it, but he couldn't understand where it was coming from. It was as though an invisible giant was taking deep breaths right next to him. In and out in gusty, snoring sighs. He got up and searched for a reason but couldn't find one. He tried telling the giant to shut up, but it made no difference. The breathing went on all night, and next morning he got lost going downstairs to breakfast. When he finally found the kitchen, Mrs Cript was already doing the washing up.

'Your eggs are cold,' she said, as she put a plate down in front of him. She didn't look pleased.

'And I've eaten all the toast,' said Mr Cript, grinning a horrible grin. There were crumbs between his square yellow teeth and butter on his chin.

'Sorry,' said Billy, 'I got lost.'

'Why don't you draw a map?' leered Mr Cript and, digging into the pocket of his shirt, he produced what looked like a length of fishing wire and began to saw away at the gaps between his molars.

That morning, Billy was very miserable indeed. The house was old and gloomy, and although it was a museum, there appeared to be no visitors. On each floor, there was a maze of corridors lined with rooms, each with signs to explain what was inside – **BEETLES**; **FLIGHTLESS BIRDS**; **MUSHROOMS AND TOADSTOOLS**. In one, there was a collection of squirrels, dozens of them, neatly labelled and stuffed. In another there was a glass cabinet containing some feathers, some beads and a comb made of narwhal horn. The comb was decorated with waves

and narwhals swimming in the same direction.
Nearby was a costume hanging on a wire frame.
'**INUIT HUNTER**' read the label beneath the
costume, and around its neck hung a necklace
of ivory animals – a seal, a bear, a whale, a
walrus, a fox with its tail missing. Billy wanted
to try it on, but he remembered what Mrs Cript
had said about not touching, so he let it be. The
empty costume seemed to be watching him.

Eventually Billy found his way
outside and wandered along the stream
his mother had pretended to be interested in,
then into a wood, where he got lost again. He
told himself it didn't matter. He was not in the
Amazon rainforest, like his dad, or at the foot
of Mount Kilimanjaro, like his mum. He was
not in a jungle full of poisonous snakes and
spiders; nevertheless he started to imagine
things. That the trees were watching him. That
the shadows were whispering to each other.
When his foot caught in a bramble, he thought

it was a hand clutching at his ankle, and within ten or fifteen minutes he felt as if he'd been lost for hours. He didn't enjoy the rustling of the leaves or the beautiful light that fell on the woodland flowers.

All he could think about were ghosts and
wild animals, until, not realising that he had
walked in a circle, he came to the kitchen
garden.

At the centre of the garden was a large rock
and, kicking it hard enough to hurt his toe, he
climbed onto it and began to cry.

3

If Billy had walked a little further, he would have found the back door and, behind it, Mrs Cript serving hot buttered crumpets as a mid-morning snack. She had made some for Billy too, but Billy didn't know this. He didn't realise how close to home he was, because the house was hidden by trees. He thought he was lost completely, and when you are lost, everything looks strange. To him, the stalks of the fennel, shooting up with their frothy tops, were like feathered spears, and even the cabbages looked threatening.

Everything seemed dangerous and
unfamiliar except the rock he was sitting
on, which was solid. An exceptionally solid,
dependable rock, with a bit of moss on it for
extra comfort. So when the rock shuddered
and rose in the air, I can forgive
him for screaming. I do
forgive him. Poor Billy!
Especially when the
rock produced a
long, enquiring
neck, with a scaly
grey head at the
end of it.

Billy screamed,
or yelled. I'll
call it a high-
pitched
yell, of the
sort many
mammals,

particularly monkeys, make when they want to explain to their friends that they are in danger. It means 'Help me!' and 'Run away!'

'Don't worry,' said the monster, 'I won't eat you.'

Which only made Billy's mouth gape wider. He stared at the scaly head and the head looked back at him. The two strangers examined one another, and slowly Billy began to relax. He had not been eaten. He had not even been bitten. The face that looked back at him wore a slight frown, but did not, I hope, seem unfriendly. The eyes blinked slowly.

'What are you?' stammered Billy.

'What do you think I am?'

Billy was not sure. He slid down and, stepping back three or four paces to take a better look – a very scientific thing to do – he gasped in admiration.

'You're a tortoise!'

And that is how we met.

'A *giant* tortoise,' I corrected him, with dignity. 'A giant Galápagos tortoise of the species *chelonoidis darwini*, and you are an ape of the species *homo sapiens*.'

'But what are you doing here?' asked Billy.

'What am *I* doing here?' I retorted. 'What are *you* doing here?'

His question struck me as rude. After all, it's my vegetable garden. But he was young. Barely out of the egg. All skinny arms and legs and big staring eyes. As I heard his story (the beginning at least) I began to understand why his manners were a little rough around the edges. Abandoned by his parents, lost, living in a house he believed to be haunted by an invisible, snoring giant. Billy told me all about himself, and I felt sorry for him. Generally, I do not speak to human beings.

When Mr Cript comes into the garden, I ignore him. I am just a rock, even when he's sitting next to me on the upturned bucket he uses as a garden chair.

But I did speak to Billy, and I have been speaking to him ever since. The story I am telling you now is his story, which I look back on with astonishment and a little pride.

'That giant,' I said, 'is probably bats.'

'Bats?'

'Roosting in the attic. When they all breathe together, it sounds like one big thing.'

'Oh,' said Billy, not sounding convinced.

'My name is Charles by the way.'

'I'm Billy,' said Billy. 'Billy S.'

'"S" for what?'

'Shaman.'

'As in spirit walker? Shape shifter? That sort of shaman?'

'Just Shaman,' said Billy, shrugging his shoulders. In those days, he didn't know any better.

'Well, I'm sorry I frightened you.'

'I'm sorry I woke you up.'

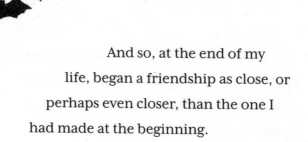

And so, at the end of my
life, began a friendship as close, or
perhaps even closer, than the one I
had made at the beginning.

24

I am a giant tortoise from the Galápagos
Islands, which were discovered a few
million years ago by my ancestors,
those brave explorers who swam across the
Pacific Ocean from South America. Why did
they make the crossing? I do not know. Did
they actually swim? Not exactly. Tortoises
are not turtles. It would be more accurate
to say that they bobbed, swept along by the
ocean currents, holding their long necks up
to breathe. Some were taken by sharks. Some
drowned. Those that survived crawled onto
the black sands of the
Galápagos, and there

have been tortoises on those
islands ever since.

There are thirteen islands in
the Galápagos group, and on
each the tortoises developed
a slightly different
shape of shell.
Some were
steep sided,
like a pepper
pot. Others
were flatter, like
an upside-down
dinner plate.

On my island, we were somewhere in the middle. Perfect, if I say so myself. I remember when I was small, following my mother and father, eating the delicious things that grew up between the volcanic rocks. We lived exactly as we pleased, without a care in the world, until one day a ship appeared and a man from that ship put me in a wooden shoebox and brought me here to England.

'What happened to your parents?' asked Billy.

I paused, because the truth is awful, and if you do not wish to hear it, close this book now. Close this book and read another.

'They were eaten,' I said.

'Eaten?' said Billy. 'Who ate them?'

'Charles did. That was the man's name.
Charles and his friends. It was a scientific
expedition, a voyage around the world, and,
well, they needed food.'

For a moment Billy could not speak. He's
a sensitive boy and I could see he was deeply
shaken, even though he wasn't particularly
fond of his own parents.

'I hate scientists,' he said. 'And explorers.'

'Yes,' I replied. 'And yet that man became
my friend.'

Billy's mouth fell open.

'Charles who ate your parents?'

'Charles who later in life became a vegetarian. I know it's hard to believe, but it's true. Some of the great explorers were very bad indeed, but Charles was kind. When I was small, no bigger than a nicely turned salad bowl, he carried me everywhere he went. I sat on his desk while he worked. We ate our meals together. Sometimes I used to wander off, and then he would come to find me and explain whatever it was I was looking at. The

specimens in his library. The glass jars in the basement, filled with things he had brought back from his expedition – tiny octopuses, fronds of seaweed – all preserved in clear alcohol. He called them his "spirit collection".'

'Because they were dead?' asked Billy, shivering.

'Don't be silly; because of the alcohol.'

'Don't you hate him?'

The question was so surprising that I
didn't know what to say. Hate Charles? It
was unthinkable – horrible! Charles, who
had taught me everything I know, whose
theories changed the world so much for the
better. Before Charles, there was darkness.
After Charles, the whole order of life, back to
the first speck of jelly, could be drawn like a
map on a flat sheet of paper. Young Charles
taught me how to think, while old Charles,
with grey hair and wrinkles of his own, kept

LETTUCE AND
TOMATO
SANDWICH
(FOR SHARING)

me company in the vegetable garden. He said
talking to me was like talking to himself, which
is how I got my name: Charles Darwin.

'No, I love him.'

'But wouldn't it have been better if you'd
never met?'

Billy was sitting cross-legged in front
of me, with his chin in his hands, as if the
answer was a simple yes or no. But it was
not straightforward. What if I had never met
Charles? What if I had never left home? Never
understood that there was a world beyond

my island, or how much it would change in my lifetime? When Charles died, he was an old man with white hair, but I was still quite a young tortoise. It is over one hundred and fifty years since we talked, and I have missed him every single day. I still listen for the sound of his footsteps walking down what he used to call 'The Thinking Path'. I can still taste the lettuce and tomato sandwiches we used to share.

But I have missed my family too. My mother and father. My brothers and sisters, aunts and uncles. My home and the delicious green things that grew there, even though I don't know what they are called and never did, because it didn't matter.

'Well?' demanded Billy, who wasn't used to watching a tortoise think.

'I don't know,' I said. 'It's a mystery.'

5

That day we talked about many things, and by the time Billy burst into the kitchen, the sun was going down. He had missed the morning crumpets. He had missed lunch and four o'clock tea. Mrs Cript had cooked fish and chips for supper, with custard and apple crumble for dessert, but her husband had eaten all the chips. All that was left of them was a greasy smear at the bottom of the pan.

'I tried to stop him,' said Mrs Cript.

'But they were too good,' Mr Cript grinned, reaching into his pocket for his fishing wire.

He had eaten all the custard too, so Billy
filled himself up with fish and dry crumble,
but he was too tired and excited from all the
talking to care. As soon as he'd finished, he
went upstairs to his bedroom, got into his
pyjamas, and was about to fall asleep, when
the invisible giant started breathing.

Billy lay awake listening, thinking about
the bats. He imagined them above his head,
hanging upside down, breathing together.
And – because his imagination is as good
as anybody else's – he imagined the spirit
collection in the basement. He thought about
the specimens Charles had brought back
from around the world, each in its glass jar,
soft or hard, with legs or without, dead and
still, or coiled in a
way that made it
seem alive. A baby
octopus, a chick, a
frog, a tapeworm,
each preserved in
clear alcohol. He
could walk along
the shelves and
read the labels,

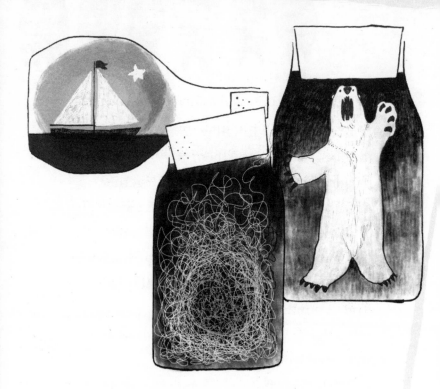

and as he went deeper into the collection, the
contents of the jars began to breathe.

Perhaps it was his own breathing that made
it seem as though the things in the jars were
breathing too. Perhaps it was the bats in the
attic, all breathing at once. Perhaps there
really was an invisible giant in the room with
him, fast asleep, its invisible mouth gaping.

Or perhaps it was Billy's gift coming to life.

Billy walked along the shelves, and as the breathing became louder, the specimens became stranger. In one jar, a tiny ship, like a ship in a bottle, sailed through snow. In another billowed a cloud of white hair. Next, a polar bear roared, with its webbed paws outstretched. Finally, alone in its glass prison, a white fox stared at him. It was not alive. It was preserved in the alcohol that the jars were filled with. It only appeared to be alive because it was so perfect.

Then it blinked and Billy woke up.

It was night-time and the giant had stopped breathing. Everything was silent. The full moon outside Billy's window sent silver light across the floor and onto the duvet. Everything was the same. Nothing had changed. He had fallen asleep without realising it, and in his imagination, he had visited the basement. None of it was real. It was just the fish and the dry apple crumble, that was all.

Then he noticed something sitting at the foot of his bed.

It was the white fox.

Through the window came a breeze that lifted its white fur. Its black eyes sparkled. They were so full of foxy intelligence, Billy felt sure it was about to speak, but it said nothing. It just stared at him, and then, with a twitch of its ears, it jumped off the bed and trotted out of the door.

6

If Billy had stayed where he was, there would be no story to tell. There would be no adventures of Billy Shaman, or new ways of looking at old things. Sometimes a single person can change everything, but Billy would not have been that person if he had not followed the fox.

So did Billy follow? He did not stop even to put his feet in his slippers, because, actually, he had no slippers, and no dressing gown either. He went out of his bedroom dressed only in the pyjamas his dad had given him for Christmas, which were decorated with cactuses. Although you may feel that these

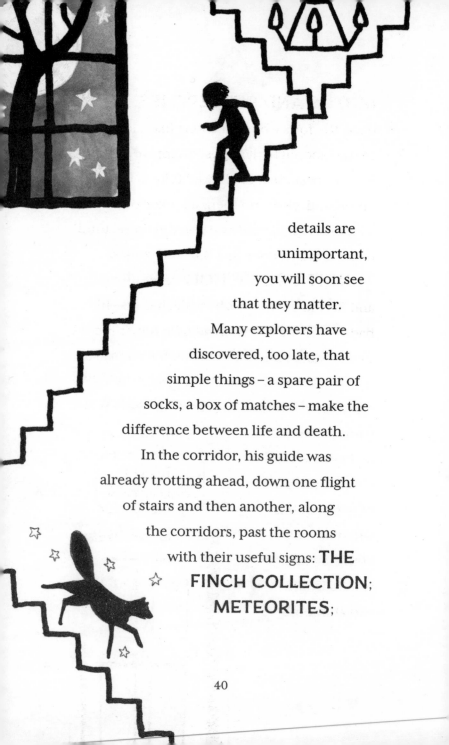

details are
unimportant,
you will soon see
that they matter.
Many explorers have
discovered, too late, that
simple things – a spare pair of
socks, a box of matches – make the
difference between life and death.
In the corridor, his guide was
already trotting ahead, down one flight
of stairs and then another, along
the corridors, past the rooms
with their useful signs: **THE
FINCH COLLECTION**;
METEORITES;

40

MOTHS AND BUTTERFLIES. In the dark, the fox's white fur shone like a lamp. In the moonlight, it almost disappeared, but it never hesitated, or allowed Billy to fall too far behind. Now and then, it looked over its shoulder to make sure he was still there, until it stopped by a door that Billy recognised.

INUIT COLLECTION, read the sign, and Billy knew what was inside, because he had visited the room already. He remembered the necklace and the comb and the empty suit of clothes. Now a breeze blew round the door, one so cold it froze his breath, and there was a noise, too, that made him think somebody had left a window open. It was not reassuring, but when he looked at the fox for some sort of explanation, it

INUIT
COLLECTION

gave nothing away. It stared back at Billy with its bright black eyes, and then, with a swish of its white tail, it walked inside.

This time, Billy hesitated, and even the greatest explorers have felt the same way as they boarded a ship, or cut the anchor rope of a hot air balloon,

or set out into the wilderness at the head of a train of mules. Behind him was the warm air of summer blowing in through the window. In front was the cold air of an unknown world. But it was the cold that drew him in.

In the corridor, Billy had stood in silence. Everything had been quiet. Inside the room, a storm raged. It filled his eyes and mouth. It roared in his ears. It swallowed the ceiling and walls. When he turned to find the door, it had gone, and the fox, his guide, had deserted him. It had disappeared into the shrieking chaos that bit through the thin cotton of his pyjamas. Now you will see what I meant earlier about the little details! What a difference a pair of slippers would have made. Or a nice warm quilted dressing gown. Or any dressing gown. But Billy had nothing but his pyjamas decorated with the cactuses his dad had

picked out specially. Cactuses! So close to the North Pole.

If Billy had jumped out of an aeroplane without a parachute, or hurled himself off a ship into the mouth of a whirlpool, he could not have been more frightened or helpless. His death was all around him. It was already happening to him. And yet, pressed into the snow at his feet, somehow resisting the ferocity of the storm, were the footprints of the fox. They led away from the place where the door had been, and when Billy followed (he had no choice) they took him to a safer place. Billy thought he saw a spark, as though a match had been struck in the whirling blizzard, and as he came closer, the spark became brighter. It was a fire, and beside the fire, a girl was sitting, wearing the clothes of an Inuit hunter.

'Who are you?' she asked.

'I'm Billy,' said Billy, but his mouth wasn't

working properly. The words came out all wrong.

'Are you a spirit?' she said. 'Are you angry with me?'

He shook his head.

'Then why are you here?'

Billy couldn't think what to say. He didn't know how. His brain had frozen.

'Get in,' said the girl. 'Get in here, or you will die.'

She offered him a corner of the blanket she was sitting beneath and moved over to make room.

7

The storm passed quickly, and when the sky cleared to a pale grey, Billy could see where he was. Around him, the snow stretched out flat to the horizon, where the sun rolled like a white wheel. It was a bleak, empty, light-headed sort of place, but at least he was no longer freezing to death. The blanket he sat beneath was made from the skin of an animal with thick fur, and Billy was grateful for it. The fire, though small, was surprisingly hot, and the blood, which had retreated to his heart for warmth, rushed joyfully back into his fingers and toes. It was agonising.

'Ouch!' he gasped.

The girl didn't say anything. She had taken a necklace from around her neck and was talking to it, all the while looking at Billy out of the corner of her eye. Billy was curious, because he was quite sure he had seen the necklace before. It was the necklace from the Inuit Collection, although, when he came to think of it, he was still in the Inuit Collection. He had not left the room. He was still in Charles Darwin's house, and yet at the same  time, he was sitting on the snow next to a girl who had certainly not been in the Inuit Collection last time he visited. And now, walking towards them across the snow, came a third person, dragging a sledge, getting bigger

and bigger until Billy could see a face. A man's
face, with skin like peeling leather.

'May I sit down?' asked the man, and when
neither Billy nor the girl answered, he sat
down anyway, with a good-natured smile.

'Nothing to say?'

He grinned a likeable grin and reached
inside his cloak, which was also made from the
skin of an animal. *A bear, possibly*, thought Billy.
A black bear.

'Here,' said the man. He handed each of
them a ball of what looked like wax, put one
into his own mouth and began to chew.

The girl watched, then popped hers into
her mouth. Immediately, tears sprang to her
eyes. She laughed.

'What is it?'

'Honey,' said the man.

'What's honey?' asked the girl.

'You know,' said the man, 'from bees.'

The girl looked as though she had never heard of bees, or tasted honey either.

'Do you have any more?' she asked.

The man laughed.

'My children like sweets too,' he said, 'but tell me your names.'

'I'm Ahnah,' said the girl, 'and this is a spirit. Be careful with him.' She pointed to Billy. 'He may be angry.'

'I'm not angry,' said Billy, 'and I'm not a spirit.'

'Then why aren't you wearing any clothes?'

She turned to the man in the bearskin cloak. 'He came out of the snow wearing nothing and sat at my fire. Probably he is looking for his body.'

'Well, if he's a spirit, he seems to like honey,' said the man, laughing. He reached behind Billy's ear and produced another of the honey balls, just as Billy had seen magicians do.

'If you tell me your name, spirit, I will tell you mine.'

'It's Billy,' said Billy, 'and I **am** wearing clothes. I'm wearing my pyjamas.'

To prove it, he opened the blanket.

'Astonishing!' said the man, admiring the cactuses. 'I have never seen finer cloth or richer dye. Where are you from?'

Billy shrugged.

'Well, this is a puzzle,' said the man, chewing the sweet he'd magicked from behind Billy's ear. 'Three strangers sitting round a fire. A brown-skinned girl in a cold place, a pale-skinned boy dressed like the prince of some hot place, and a travelling Greek, each with a story to tell. Who will go first?'

Nobody said anything.

'Very well,' said the man, 'let it be me. But wait, my manners – where have I put them?'

He pretended to look around, searching inside his cloak and patting the snow.

He grinned his likeable grin.

'My name is Pytheas,' he said, producing two more sweets out of thin air, 'sailor, astronomer, explorer. My home is faraway Massalia. I am searching for the edge of the world, and I believe I have found it. Here, where the sun shines at midnight.'

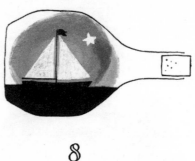

8

N ot long ago, Billy would have said he wasn't interested in explorers, or astronomers either, since astronomy is a science. He had never read about the adventures of Marco Polo in China or read a history of the telescope (or the microscope). But now he was interested, and Ahnah seemed interested too. They sat around the fire, all three of them, and the snow was like a sheet of white paper waiting to be written on.

'Do you like magic?' asked Pytheas.

They nodded.

'And would you call this magic?' asked Pytheas, reaching into his robes for a handkerchief, stuffing it into his closed fist, then pulling out one of a different colour entirely.

'It is a trick,' said Ahnah.

'Do another,' said Billy.

'Very well,' said Pytheas, putting the original handkerchief back inside his cloak. 'What if I were to tell you that I have sailed across the ocean using only the stars to guide me? And that by the magic of my astronomy, I have made islands rise from the water to meet me?'

'That's not magic,' said Billy. 'That's navigation.'

'But it *feels* like magic,' said Pytheas, 'when you are alone on your boat. When the cheese you have eaten for a month is full of maggots and you have drunk every drop of your fresh water. You begin to think that perhaps the gods have deserted you, or that there are no gods, only the dark and the ocean and the monsters that are certainly in it.

You wonder if the star you thought was the Pole star is nothing of the kind, and of no more importance to a lost sailor than the millions of other winking lights up there. No forest could be more terrifying! No cave so frightful! But just as you are convinced there is no hope, you see something that blots out the stars completely, a huge shape. Is it a sea dragon? Or Death himself? Your heart freezes. It stops. Then the sound of the waves changes and you know that what you have prayed for has come true. Land! Where you had prayed to find land...

'A feeling comes into you. There is nothing else like it. Nothing to equal it. Relief! Astonishment! Wonder! Now *that* is magic.'

Billy felt like clapping his hands, and even Ahnah looked impressed.

'Have you travelled a very long way?' she asked.

'Very,' said Pytheas, using his knuckles to draw a line in the snow.

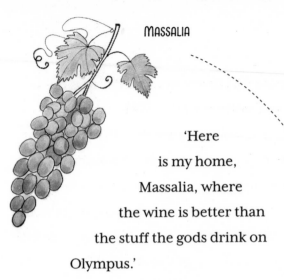

'Here
is my home,
Massalia, where
the wine is better than
the stuff the gods drink on
Olympus.'

He drew another line.

'From Massalia, I sailed across the sea to where the Britons live. Look!'

From his sledge, he took a metal cup.

'It is made of tin, a gift from the Britons closest to my own country. They gave me a plate too.'

He produced one with a flourish.

'I sailed on, to the west and north,

BRITONS

up the coast of that country and across the sea.
I survived many storms and saw wonderful
creatures. I met many interesting people,
including a tribe of red-haired barbarians
who gave me this.'

He rolled back his sleeve and showed them
the silhouette of a whale, tattooed into his skin
with blue ink.

'It was painful,' he admitted, 'but I am
pleased with the result. I also met seals and
mermaids, though sometimes it is hard to tell
the difference.'

He grinned.

'I got these sweets from an island so far
north of my home that the sun sets for only
a short time each night. They have bees
there and bread. They gave me this.'

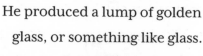

He produced a lump of golden
glass, or something like glass.

'It is called amber,'
he said. 'It comes

from the sea. At home, it's as precious as real gold, but in that place, it's so common they use it like firewood.'

He tossed it on the fire, and Billy reached to snatch it out, but Pytheas only laughed and grabbed his wrist, then showed him the amber he had been holding in his other hand all along.

'How did you do that?' asked Billy, rubbing his arm.

'Much practice,' said Pytheas. 'Long hours at sea. It fills the time when there is nothing else to do.'

He looked serious.

'The people who gave me this amber were farmers, but I do not think there are farmers here. I have left my boat back there in the ice, stuck fast. I walked here across the frozen sea. Surely, nothing can grow here. No wheat. No trees. Although I see you are burning something.'

He glanced at them.

'Which of you can tell me what it is? Who is the native here and who is the stranger? Here, at the edge of the world?'

'This is my place,' said Ahnah.
'I was born here, and I am

burning seal fat. I am waiting for my
grandmother, and if you want to see
real magic, wait for her with me.
She is a shaman.'

9

When Billy heard his own name, he paid no attention to it. He was used to being Billy Shaman. It was just what he was called. Billy S – instead of Billy G or Billy W – to make a difference between him and the other two Billys in his class.

He was more interested in the man sitting opposite, who was listening to Ahnah with a smile. A man who had arrived by ship from a distant country, without any crew, and seen dragons and mermaids and filled his pockets with amber. But the explorer was curious.

'What is a shaman?' asked Pytheas.

'A spirit traveller,' said Ahnah, raising her

chin and looking down her nose. 'A soul doctor. A person who can talk to animals and even to the dead. My grandmother is a far more powerful magician than you.'

'And what is that you have in your hands?'

'Nothing to you,' said Ahnah, holding her necklace tighter.

'May I see it?'

'No,' said Ahnah, 'it's mine.'

'Please,' said Pytheas.

He spoke softly. He was not a trickster or a boaster any more. He had come a long way and he was tired. Ahnah studied him, and he held her gaze. His face told her that she could trust him.

'Thank you,' he said as she gave him the necklace. 'What is it made of?'

'Walrus ivory,' she said.

'And is it a magical object?' asked Pytheas.

'It's a spirit necklace,' said Ahnah. 'My grandfather carved it for me.'

'Is he a shaman too?'

'He is dead.'

Pytheas nodded and bent closer to the
necklace.

'It is beautiful. What does it do?'

'It protects me from the souls of the animals
that my family have hunted and killed. The
seal, the walrus, the bear, the whale, the fox.
In case they are angry with us.'

Billy could see the carved animals strung
along the necklace as Pytheas inspected them,
tracing the shape of them with his fingers.

'Which is your favourite?' asked Pytheas.

'The seal,' said Ahnah, and as she said it, her
face came to life, her eyes sparkling, almost
as if by saying the word she was becoming the
animal. 'The seal is so happy.' She smiled.

'The seal,' said Pytheas. 'Yes, I love the seal
too.' He cupped the necklace in his hands.

'But there is no carving of a man here,' he
added in a whisper, as if disappointed. 'No

64

human being. And what is more dangerous
than a human being?'

He looked at them, and when he opened his
hands, the necklace had gone.

'Give it back!' said Ahnah, jumping to her
feet.

'Give what back?' asked Pytheas, and the
trickster had returned.

'My necklace! Give me my necklace. You had it. Where have you put it?'

Pytheas only smiled.

'Just a trick,' he said softly. 'Don't be angry. Sit and listen to me a little longer.'

'I will not,' said Ahnah. 'I don't trust you.'

Pytheas shrugged.

'Look over there,' he said, pointing behind her. 'What do you see?'

Ahnah turned quickly.

'The snow,' she said.

'The snow,' he repeated. 'Now what if I were to say that to the south of here, where I come from, the sun shines so hotly that there is only snow on the mountain tops? The grapes are purple. The grass is green. Children swim like fish in the rivers, or bask on the rocks, and when they come home, they eat so much bread and honey they have to be careful not to burst.'

'I would say,' said Ahnah, 'that they are greedy children.'

'But aren't you interested to see it for yourself?' said Pytheas. 'Don't you wonder what the world is like outside this little circle we are sitting in? This little fire? Don't you want to know?'

'Give me back my necklace,' said Ahnah, 'or I will call my grandmother.'

'I will give it back,' said Pytheas, 'if you promise to come with me.'

'Give it back to me *now!*' said Ahnah, and Billy jumped up too.

'Are you looking for this?' asked Pytheas, and in his hand he held a knife. Ahnah was staring at the empty scabbard at her belt, and her face looked empty too. She was amazed.

'You are a demon,' she gasped, as Pytheas rose to his feet. He was very tall and the black bearskin cloak made him seem huge, although his face was thin and serious again. He looked hungry.

'Only a man,' he said, stepping forward. At the same moment, the snow seemed to gather itself and stand, making the shape of a bear even taller than Pytheas and more terrifying. The trickster in the black bearskin cloak was dwarfed by the living white polar bear behind him, opening its mouth to roar, showing its teeth and dark tongue.

And now, thought Billy, *I am going to die*.

He did not just think it. His whole body *knew* it. He heard Pytheas shout in horror, saw the polar bear lunge with its wide-open mouth and outstretched claws... And then it was as if a freezing wave crashed over him,

sweeping everything away, the bear, the snow, the white wheel of the sun, and when he opened his eyes, he was back in Charles Darwin's house, lying in bed. It took him a while to realise. The sheets, the pillow, the cracked plaster of the ceiling, the morning sunshine. Not a cold sun, but a warm yellow sun, with a nice breeze blowing in through the window, bringing the smell of the summer garden and the sound of birds singing.

There was no doubt about it. The room was real and he was really lying in it. Somewhere in the house, a grandfather clock was chiming eight o'clock. But just as Billy was beginning to believe that the adventure of the previous night had been a dream (and was celebrating the fact) he noticed there was somebody at the end of his bed, curled up like a dog or cat and fast asleep.

'Ow!' said Ahnah, when he prodded her with his toe. 'Stop kicking!'

10

It may surprise you to know that the first thing on Billy's mind was not how Ahnah came to be lying at the end of his bed, but what Mr and Mrs Cript might say if they found out. How would he explain who she was, or how she had got there? Probably Mr Cript would call the police and then what would he do? The police would phone his parents, who would be disappointed and angry. Billy could imagine their faces. His dad torn away from the Amazon rainforest in the middle of his hunt for carnivorous flytraps. His mum halfway up a mountain.

'How could you do this to us, Billy?' his dad would say.

'Why are you so selfish?' his mum would add.

'After all the things we've done for you,' they would say together, while the policeman nodded and got out his notepad.

Then the real questions would begin, and Billy would not have any answers. Probably he would go to prison.

Meanwhile, Ahnah had woken up and was staring at him.

'Is this the spirit world?' she asked. 'Am I dead?'

'Not unless the bear killed us,' said Billy.

'What bear?' said Ahnah.

'The huge polar bear,' said Billy. 'Don't you remember? The gigantic, ferocious polar bear that attacked Pytheas. It must have been stalking him all the way from his boat. I bet it tore him to pieces. I even feel sorry for him.'

Ahnah snorted.

'That wasn't a bear,' she said. 'That was my grandmother.'

'Your grandmother is a bear?'

'The bear is her spirit animal,' said Ahnah, with a backward tilt of her head. 'Like yours is a fox.'

'What fox?' said Billy.

'The fox you came with. You don't have to pretend.'

The fox! He had completely forgotten about it.

'Come on,' he whispered, 'I've got something to show you.'

Quietly,
because he was
afraid that Mr and
Mrs Cript would hear
them, he led Ahnah down
the stairs and along the
corridor, the same way the fox
had led him the night before. The
door was still ajar, but inside the room,
there was no blizzard. Everything was back
to normal – the narwhal's horn on the wall,
the glass cabinet beneath the window,
the costume of clothes that Ahnah
now stood face-to-empty-face
with, as though she was
looking at the ghost of
herself in a mirror.

'What is this place?' she asked.

'It's a museum.'

'What's a museum?'

'A place to put things in.'

'What sort of things?'

He shrugged.

'Look!' Ahnah exclaimed. 'That's my necklace! How did it get here?'

'Ssshh!' hissed Billy. 'Not so loud.'

'But it is. It's my necklace. Look at it!'

She reached up and took it from around the costume's neck.

'Put it back!' said Billy. 'Can't you read? It says DO NOT TOUCH.'

'The fox has lost his tail.'

'It can't be your necklace,' said Billy. 'Read the label. It's over two thousand years old.'

'*You* read the label!' snapped Ahnah, who had gone bright red. 'It's my necklace and that is my grandmother's comb.'

She pointed to the glass cabinet, where the

comb lay with the feathers and beads, then turned on Billy fiercely.

'How did it get here?'

Billy didn't know. He didn't know how the necklace was on the costume or the comb was in the cabinet, any more than he understood how Ahnah had arrived at the foot of his bed, or how he had visited her in the first place. He just knew she was speaking too loudly.

'Please,' he said, 'keep your voice down.'

'You keep your voice down!'

'If you don't keep quiet,' said Billy, trying hard to keep calm, 'Mr and Mrs Cript will call the police.'

'And I shall call my grandmother,' shouted Ahnah, 'and when she comes, she will eat the police and she will eat you too. Oh, she will be so angry! You will see her hair grow very long.'

IVORY COMB

AMBER BEADS

FEATHERS FROM
ARCTIC TERN

NARWHAL'S HORN

INUIT CLOTHES
& IVORY NECKLACE
C. 350BCE
PLEASE DO NOT TOUCH

It was a strange threat, but Billy let it go. Everything was going so badly wrong it made him dizzy. His whole world, perfectly round, spinning quietly in space, had turned inside out.

'Wait here!' he told Ahnah. 'Don't move.'

When he returned ten minutes later, he was relieved to find that she was where he'd left her, staring at the narwhal's horn.

'What have you got there?' she asked, as though the paper bags he was carrying might be stuffed with the missing narwhal.

'Sandwiches,' he said. 'Now, please, come with me. I have someone I want to introduce you to.'

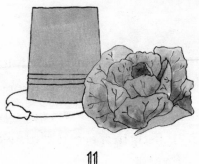

11

By 'someone', Billy meant me, of course, but I was not in a good mood. The night before, I hadn't slept well, and when I finally did, I dreamed disturbing dreams. I was the wrong sort of tortoise, with a bucket instead of a shell. Charles came to visit me, but he was not the right Charles, and when he offered me a sandwich, it wriggled. It was a horrible dream, but the next was worse, because it was lovely. I was back on my island with my family, and I was happy.

It's a dream based, I am fairly sure, on a real memory. I was sitting in a nice pool of warm mud with about a hundred other tortoises,

blowing bubbles. My mother and father were there, my uncles and aunts, my grandparents, warming up in the volcanic mud. As usual, I woke with a wonderful feeling of being surrounded by others like me, with that same feeling of blissful ignorance I had when I was small. Back then, I didn't know there were other tortoises on other islands, with shells different to my own, or that beyond those islands was a whole world with all kinds of astonishing creatures in it. My family was enough. The warm mud we sat in. The paths we made, as we followed the rain that caused green things to grow. Home.

I was so happy that when Billy and Ahnah came running into the garden, I didn't want to wake up. I wanted to stay where I belonged, but I couldn't, because somebody was banging on my shell.

'He looks like a rock,' shouted Billy, 'but he's actually a giant tortoise. Look, Charles, I've brought you a sandwich!'

When I finally poked my head out of my shell to see what was happening, I hissed, which for a tortoise is close to biting. But then I saw Ahnah's face.

'Don't worry,' I said grumpily, 'I won't eat you.'

'Are you a monster?' she asked. I suppose the closest thing she had seen to me was a walrus.

'Do I look like a monster?'

'Yes,' she said.

'Well, I'm not,' I assured her.

'He's a giant tortoise,' said

Billy, 'from the Galápagos Islands. *Adanoidis* something.'

'*Chelonoidis*,' I corrected him, '*darwini*.'

'He was kidnapped by an explorer,' explained Billy, 'like Pytheas tried to kidnap us.'

Ahnah's eyes were so wide I could see the whites all the way around.

'Isn't that right, Charles?' continued Billy.

'I suppose so,' I said. 'In a way.'

Ahnah flinched as I spoke, and she followed every move I made. I could see there was no point in trying to find out what was going on until I had calmed her down, so I asked Billy what was in his sandwiches.

'Lettuce and tomato,' said Billy.

'Then might I trouble you for a few shreds of lettuce?'

I let him feed it to me until Ahnah stopped staring and even began to look a little envious.

'Do you like these red things?' she asked eventually.

LETTUCE & TOMATO SANDWICH RECIPE

BUTTER DISH

SALT & PEPPER

'Tomatoes?' I replied. 'I am particularly fond of tomatoes.'

Which is true, although it is a long, long time since somebody offered to share the tomatoes from their sandwich with me. Now Ahnah fed me hers, slice by slice, at first

carefully, snatching her fingers away, then
with more confidence, until there were none
left.

Then, frowning and blushing furiously, she
summoned her courage and asked in a voice
that was almost impossible to hear, 'Please, oh
tortoise, may I stroke your nose?'

'Just this once,' I said.

So Ahnah stroked my nose, and a little
while later, she and Billy told me their story.

12

What a story it was! And how well
they told it! Not in the way that
Pytheas the Greek might have
done, gracefully, with poetical phrases, but in
a rush, correcting and talking over each other.
The fox! The storm! The stranger! The bear!
Several times I had to stop them and ask them
to repeat something, which they did, adding
new details, contradicting each other – 'he had
a knife' – 'that was *my* knife' – fighting over the
right way of saying things that meant nothing
to me. In short, talking as human beings talk
when they are telling the truth.

When they had finished, they both looked

at me expectantly, as if I would know exactly what to do. As if I could explain what had happened to them and return Ahnah to where she came from. Of course, I could do nothing of the sort. I am a giant tortoise with my four scaly feet firmly planted on the ground. I have lived for a long time and seen all sorts of things. But even the great Charles Darwin (I mean the human Charles Darwin) would not have understood how Billy had travelled two thousand years back in time, or how Ahnah had travelled forwards with him. Or how the necklace in Ahnah's hand could be yellow with age while the hand that held it was still young.

I could imagine Charles's face, frowning at the strangeness of it, so I began with what I knew, which is something Charles also believed in. *Start with the facts*, he used to tell people. *Keep it simple!* So I told them about Pytheas, the man in the black cloak. Pytheas the great explorer, astronomer and sailor,

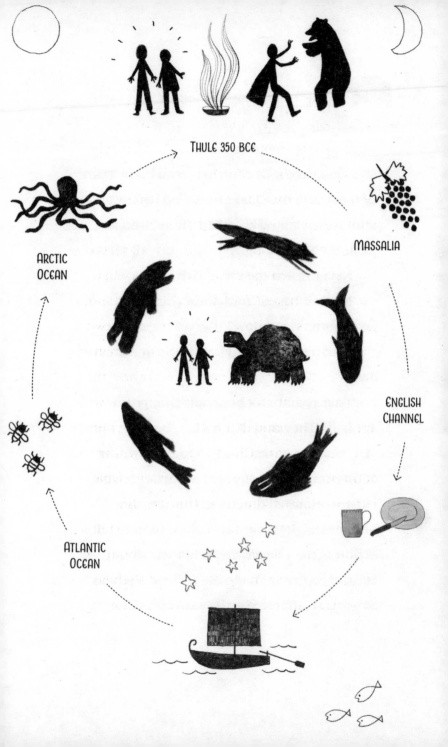

who long ago sailed further from home than any of his people had ever sailed before and discovered a land he called Thule, which means 'the utter north'.

'Never heard of it,' said Billy.

'Neither have I,' said Ahnah heatedly. 'And I live there.'

'I bet he made the whole thing up,' sneered Billy.

'That's what a lot of people thought,' I replied. 'They called him a liar, because they had never seen the things he said he'd seen. Most of what he told them was true though. Pytheas claimed the sun in the utter north shone at night as well as in the day, and it does. He drew the stars as they really do appear inside the Arctic Circle. He noticed that the tides were affected by the moon, which they

are. He discovered lots of things besides, which is why people talk about him today. He was one of the first of the great explorers.'

'He *is* a liar!' said Billy. 'And a thief too.'

'He stole my necklace,' said Ahnah, clutching it as if Pytheas might try to magic it away again.

'He tried to kidnap us.'

'And force us into his boat.'

'And take us home with him.'

'Probably to prove that he had been where he said he'd been,' I suggested.

'He's a bad man,' said Ahnah. 'I hope my grandmother ate every last bit of him.'

'But she can't have,' I pointed out. 'Because he lived to tell his story. He sailed back home to Massalia with your necklace, and as far as I know, he lived to a ripe old age. For a human.'

They considered
this disappointing news,
while I wondered what to say next.
I couldn't think of anything useful. I had
already told them everything I knew.

'What do you call the place you live in?' I
asked Ahnah.

'I don't call it anything,' she said angrily.
'It's not a person! It's the place where my
family live and my friends and my dogs. It's
where I know how to do things and where
things are, instead of... this.'

She waved her hands at the cabbage stalks
and the upturned bucket that Mr Cript
sometimes sat on when he was drinking his tea.

'I want to go home!'

She was close to tears and I did

not blame her. Who does not dream of home
when they are feeling lonely and frightened?
If home is safe and friendly, which is what
home means. In Ahnah's case, I could see no
hope of her ever returning, because she did
not know where her home was. Because it was
lost somewhere in the past, in the snow and
ice at the top of the world. Because the man
who had stolen her necklace was dead and
the book he wrote was lost too, along with the
map of his voyage. These days, when people
talk about Thule, they mean somewhere far
north, but they don't know exactly where.
Perhaps Pytheas sailed to Greenland, or
Iceland, or Norway. Nobody knows, and even
if the lost map was discovered, Ahnah would
still not find what she was looking for, because
her home was not only a long way away, but a
long time ago. The people she knew and loved
were gone now. Her grandmother, her family,

the dogs that pulled her sledge – dead for over two thousand years.

She didn't understand, yet. She still believed they were just out of sight, where she had left them. She had only been gone a moment. But I understood and it broke my heart.

Billy was not daunted though. Something about the adventure had changed him, so that the boy who had come to see me the day before – a little shy, scared of ghosts, perhaps a little like a ghost himself – had become bold, with a glint in his eye.

'Well, I'm glad you're here, Ahnah,' he said, jumping to his feet. 'It was boring without you. Come on, let's explore the forest!'

13

illy and Ahnah jumped up and off they went, into the trees, just as children have been doing for billions of years, whoever they happen to be, leaving their parents and uncles and aunts to grumble. Youngsters have always been like that. One moment, they are frantic because they are lost or cold or hungry. The next, they're bouncing up and down shouting their heads off, playing some new game.

'Look at this!' they bellow. 'Look at that!'

Rushing around like nobody's business, making a hullabaloo, as if nothing else mattered but whatever it

96

is they were doing right there and then.

'That's a marsh orchid,' Billy said, pointing to the marsh orchid.

He said it a little sulkily, remembering the last time he'd seen it, but Ahnah was so impressed it cheered him up.

'Oh!' she said. 'And what's that?'

'A butterfly,' said Billy, trying to remember what kind of butterfly, but it didn't matter, because Ahnah had never seen any sort of butterfly. She chased it along the stream until something else caught her eye.

'What's that?' she kept asking. 'What's this?'

Soon she had forgotten she was lost and Billy was having a wonderful time. When he didn't know the name of something, he made it up.

'That's a rhinoceros,' he said, when Ahnah pointed to an insect crouching on a water reed.

'A rhinoceros,' repeated Ahnah.

'Actually, it's a dragonfly,' said Billy, laughing.

'Is it?' said Ahnah. She didn't care what it was called. She was in love with it.

'Come on,' said Billy, and off they went, following the stream under the trees.

'Let's see if we can find where it comes from,' said Billy.

'Wait a moment,' said Ahnah, 'I have to take off my jacket.'

STREAM

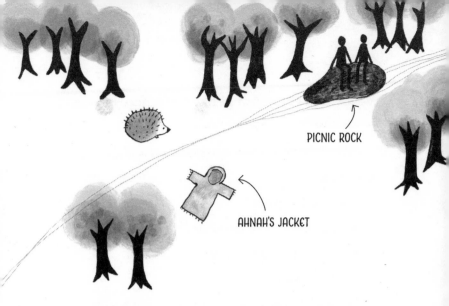

PICNIC ROCK

AHNAH'S JACKET

They ate their lunch sitting on a warm grey stone, miles from the house. The stream rushed past them on either side. The lunchtime sandwiches had got wet, but it didn't matter. They tasted delicious.

'I'm going for a swim,' said Billy.

It was evening by the time they reached the spring that the stream came from, deep inside the wood, which had become a forest, with trees so thick that the sun could hardly push through the leaves. Ahnah kept stroking the tree trunks.

'We don't have things like this where I come from,' she said.

'What do you build your houses with?' asked Billy.

'Ice,' said Ahnah.

'But aren't you always cold?'

She thought a moment.

'Yes,' she said.

They didn't discuss what they were going to do next, or how Ahnah would return, or what Billy would say to Mr and Mrs Cript. He had forgotten all about them, because he was enjoying himself so much, and Ahnah was enjoying herself too. She had forgotten she was in trouble, lost in time, with no way home. They were both having an adventure.

On their way back, they stopped by a pool to eat the last of the biscuits. Ahnah saw a fish hiding under a rock.

'Come,' she said, dipping her hand into the water. The fish stayed where it was.

'My grandmother can call fish,' she explained. 'But I haven't learned how to. It is an art.'

'Can she really turn into a polar bear?' asked Billy.

'Of course,' said Ahnah. 'Didn't you see? Also a walrus. But when she's really angry, she becomes the sea witch, Sedna, and that's when her hair grows long.'

Billy told her about the invisible giant and the dream he'd had about the spirit collection and what had been in the jars. The ship, the hair, the bear, the fox.

'You dreamed it and then it happened?'

'Sort of.'

'And the fox came to be your guide?'

'Yes.'

'Probably that snoring giant is all the spirits breathing together,' she said. 'And you can hear it because you're a shaman.'

'I'm not a shaman,' he said, 'it's just my name. It doesn't mean anything.'

Ahnah was no longer listening. They had been walking through the forest, which was filled with trees older than the house itself, and flowers from all over the world. Sunshine made coins of gold dance around their feet and on their faces. Everything was thrilling, alive and magical, waiting to be discovered.

But then a man Billy did not recognise stepped out from behind a tree. It was not Pytheas, or Mr Cript, or his dad, returned suddenly from Brazil. The man was wearing a handkerchief on his head and the bottoms of his trousers were wet. The expression on his face was extremely serious.

'Is your name Billy?' he asked.

'Yes,' replied Billy.

'And is this your friend?'

Ahnah nodded.

'And where did you get that necklace?'

Ahnah couldn't think of anything to say.

'Right then,' said the man and, producing his identity card, he explained that he was a plain-clothes police detective and that they were both under arrest.

14

Probably you will be wondering how a plain-clothes detective came to be hiding behind a tree in Charles Darwin's garden in the first place, and I will explain.

That morning, while Billy and Ahnah had been upstairs in the Inuit room, Mr and Mrs Cript had been downstairs eating their breakfast. It will not surprise you to hear that Mr Cript had eaten all the toast.

'You're a very greedy man,' Mrs Cript told him.

'I know it,' he admitted, using his finger to wipe up the last of the marmalade from his plate.

TOAST RACK

MARMALADE

It upset Mrs Cript that her husband was
always eating Billy's food, and so when Billy
appeared and asked if she could make him
some sandwiches, she was happy to help. She
was only surprised that he needed so many.

'I'll be out for lunch too,' said Billy, filling
a water bottle and pocketing some biscuits. 'I
won't be back until supper time.'

'That boy is up to something,' said Mr Cript,
when Billy had gone.

'Nonsense,' said Mrs Cript. 'Whatever makes you say so?'

'I'm a man of the world,' said Mr Cript, closing one eye and squinting at the ceiling with the other. 'And as a man of the world, I say that Billy is up to no good.'

'Rubbish,' snorted Mrs Cript. She was used to her husband saying unpleasant things behind people's backs. Quite often, he said them to their faces too. In Mr Cript's opinion,

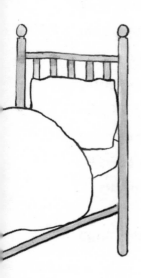

almost everybody was up to something. It didn't mean they were. All the same, as soon as Mrs Cript had tidied away breakfast, she went up to Billy's bedroom. She told herself it was because the sheets needed changing, but actually she wanted to snoop.

Immediately, she noticed a pair of sealskin gloves lying on the floor.

'Now where did these come from?' she asked herself, and she hurried downstairs to the Inuit Collection.

Unlike Mr Cript, Mrs Cript liked to think the best of people, and so she was relieved to see that the Inuit costume's gloves were still where they were meant to be, at either end of the sleeves of the Inuit jacket. She told herself that Billy was a good boy. A little strange perhaps. The eyes. The hair. A nice boy though, who just happened to have a pair of sealskin gloves lying about in his bedroom. She did not know where he had got them, but she was sure he would have an explanation, and she was just breathing a sigh of relief when she noticed that the necklace – the priceless Inuit necklace, hung with animals carved from walrus ivory – was gone.

Mrs Cript was not an ordinary housekeeper. She was a professional curator, which is a person who looks after and

organises museums.

She was also a doctor of anthropology, which is the study of the history of human beings, and had taught at several universities. Mr Cript knew a lot about plants, which is why he spent so much time in the garden, but his wife understood the museum, not just to dust and polish, more as a jigsaw puzzle in her mind. When she noticed that a piece of that puzzle was missing, she gasped. The walrus ivory necklace was over two thousand years old. It had been loaned to the museum by a collector. How would she explain to the collector that it had gone missing? And could it really have been Billy who'd stolen it? She didn't want to think so, but she couldn't help it.

She thought of so many things

at once that she couldn't decide which to think about properly, so at first, she did nothing. She went about her morning chores, and it was only when Mr Cript came in for his lunch that she told him what had happened.

'Mr Cript...' she began, and as she explained, his smile became broader.

'You see?' he said. 'What did I tell you? Billy's up to no good. And I'll tell you a second thing...' He winked and took the sealskin gloves from the pocket of his wife's apron. 'He has an accomplice.'

Mr Cript was so pleased with his theory that he did not pause to taste his lunch before phoning the police.

15

When the police arrived at the house, they took out their notebooks and asked the sorts of questions that policemen do. They were not wearing uniforms. They were in their ordinary clothes, because they did not want to attract attention to themselves, although you could tell they were policemen by looking at their boots. They wanted to know why Billy was staying at the house and how long he had been gone. They listened to Mr Cript's theory about a criminal accomplice and asked why the thieves would be wearing sealskin gloves in the middle of summer.

When they had finished asking questions, they began hunting for clues. The policeman who was most interested in natural history asked if Mrs Cript would show him around the house, while the policeman who most fancied a walk in the countryside said he would go into the garden to see if he could find any trace of the thief. Though he warned that Billy was probably long gone, taking his accomplice with him. If there had ever been an accomplice.

The policeman who was interested in natural history had a wonderful afternoon. Mrs Cript gave him a proper tour

of the museum, starting with the Inuit Collection and ending in the library. She showed him Charles Darwin's study, where Charles had written his most famous books. The policeman was in awe. He sat in Charles Darwin's chair. He looked at pages that Charles Darwin had written over a hundred and fifty years ago. He leaned very close to study the ink on the page.

'Please don't touch,' said Mrs Cript.

The policeman blushed.

Meanwhile, the policeman who fancied a walk in the countryside was sitting on the rock that Billy and Ahnah had eaten their lunch on, with his trousers rolled up to his knees and a knotted handkerchief on his head to keep the sun off. It was a beautiful afternoon. The stream smelled of wet stone. The water made a lovely gurgling sound. It made him sleepy, and although he knew he was on duty, he didn't see any harm in closing his eyes for a moment, to let the sunshine wash over him.

It was so refreshing that he lost any sense of time, and when he woke up it was much, much later. He jumped to his feet and splashed back across the river, then ran along the bank to where he'd left his boots, failing

Z
Z
Z
KNOTTED
← HANDKERCHIEF
(TO KEEP THE
SUN OFF)

to notice a sealskin jacket that somebody had tossed onto the bank earlier. Somehow, he had been asleep for hours! Probably he would be sacked! He could already hear the chief constable shouting at him, and all because he loved long walks in the countryside.

He ran back through the trees around the house, wondering what he was going to do when he was not a policeman any more, and what he would tell his girlfriend, who was a geography teacher. He ran so fast that he nearly missed the suspects altogether. A boy who fitted the description Mr Cript had given. Dark hair. Big green eyes. Rabbity expression. There was a girl with him too, dressed in sealskin trousers and a sealskin shirt. Around her neck was the walrus ivory necklace.

A minute later, Billy and Ahnah were under arrest.

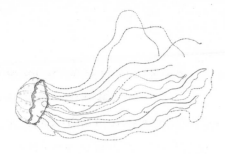

16

By the time the policeman returned with Billy and Ahnah, the policeman who enjoyed natural history (who I shall now call 'the first policeman') was beginning to feel at home. He had completed his tour of the house and was drinking coffee with Mr and Mrs Cript in the library. He had eaten his supper in Charles Darwin's dining room and imagined the great man sitting where he sat. It was almost as if he *was* Charles Darwin, helping himself to mustard, pondering theories that would change the world. Where does life come from? How old is it? Can jellyfish think? It was a nice feeling, so he was disappointed when the second policeman returned, looking rather sunburned, with Billy and Ahnah walking in front of him.

'What's that you've got on your head?' asked the first policeman. He was the most important of the two, which was why he was asking the questions.

'A knotted handkerchief,' said the second policeman. 'I found these two hiding in the woods. The boy and his friend.'

'We weren't hiding,' protested Billy. 'We were having a walk.'

'So you say,' scoffed Mr Cript.

The first policeman sighed. He had enjoyed pretending he was Charles Darwin. He reached for his notebook.

'Name?' he asked Billy.

'Billy,' said Billy. 'Billy Shaman.'

'And you, miss?'

'Ahnah,' said Ahnah.

'Ahnah what?'

'What do you mean, "what"?'

'What's your second name?'

'I don't have a second name. Sometimes my grandmother calls me "little pup", but nobody else does. It's because she used to look after me when I was a baby.'

She looked very small where she stood, beside the policeman. Her head didn't reach

even as high as his notebook,
and for a moment, everybody felt
sorry for her. They were all thinking of her as a
baby, being looked after by her grandmother,
and it made them want to look after her too.
All except for Mr Cript.

'What would your grandmother say if
she knew you'd been stealing other people's
necklaces?' he said nastily.

'I didn't steal it. My grandfather made it for
me.'

'So where's your grandfather?'

'He's dead.'

'How convenient.'

Ahnah looked stunned. She didn't know
what to say. Billy just felt sick. It was exactly
as he had imagined from the moment he'd
found Ahnah curled up on his bed. He'd
known the police would come, and now here
they were. They would want to know where
Ahnah's family lived and when she explained,

they would not believe her. They would put her in an orphanage; or worse, they would think she was mad. The only way Billy could save her was to say it was he who had stolen the necklace, and then the police would phone his parents and his parents would come back from their holidays. But they wouldn't be able to help him. Probably they wouldn't even want to

Dear Billy,
We are still very disappointed in you.
Love,
Mum and Dad

BILLY SHAMAN

PRISON

help him. They would shake their heads as he was led away to prison and get on with their own adventures. If he was lucky, they would send him the occasional postcard.

Billy could see it so clearly, and it was all Mr Cript's fault. Mr Cript, who always wanted to think the worst of people. Who looked so like a gargoyle that Billy wanted to shout it out loud.

'*You're a gargoyle, Mr Cript! A gargoyle! Take a look at yourself in the mirror!*' He wished he really was a shaman, so that he could do something dreadful. Turn himself into a sea monster. Summon a swarm of killer bees. Call up a storm, with thunder and lightning, so that Mr Cript could see just how angry Billy was. He was so angry that he forgot he couldn't do it, and outside the window, lightning began to flicker.

Nobody noticed but Billy. The policemen were standing under the chandelier with Ahnah between them. Mr and Mrs Cript were arguing. They did not see the flashes outside, or the bookshelves inside begin to glow. Or the shadows that flew out of them, small birds, insects, bats, as if the pictures inside the books were coming to life. They filled the

air so thickly that Billy could not see through them. It was as though the whole library was turning inside out, but nobody paid any attention, because they did not have Billy's gift. He saw them with his spirit eye, lifting, falling, swarming. It was like a living curtain, and when the curtain parted, he saw an old woman, sitting by a fire.

Billy stood on one side of the room and the old lady sat at the other, at the end of a row of bookcases. But Billy could hardly see the books. The library had dimmed down, while the old lady was lit up by the fire On the other side of the fire lay a man, with a blanket over him. It was Pytheas.

The woman turned and looked straight at him.

'Who's that?' she asked. She peered along the dark avenue of books, as if she was blind. She was dressed in sealskin, decorated with patches in the shape of suns and hands.

'I can feel you,' she said, 'but I can't see you. What are you?'

Billy couldn't think of anything to say.

'Are you a demon?' She stood up. 'Do you know where Ahnah is?'

'Yes, I do,' said Billy. 'She's here with me and she's in trouble.'

'Then let me come!'

'How?'

Billy could see the old woman's face lit by the fire, the deep, slanting wrinkles on her forehead, her shining wide-set eyes, her nose like a beak.

'Invite me in,' she said. 'Don't be afraid. Open your heart to me and I will come.'

Billy was afraid. He remembered the bear. He saw the dark, fierce eyes. But he did as he was told.

'All right,' he said, 'come.'

'Thank you,' said Ahnah's grandmother, and she stepped over the fire, from her world into Billy's.

17

Inside the library, the policemen were wondering what to do with Ahnah. It was complicated and uncomfortable, and they didn't want her to hear what they were talking about. They spoke in whispers, leaning their heads close together while she watched them.

None of them noticed the old woman, walking softly down the long corridor. The fire had disappeared the moment she stepped over it. Pytheas had disappeared too. Now she was in Billy's place, but at first, only Billy knew it, and he was worried that he had made a mistake. The old lady walked quietly, on the flats of her feet, stalking her own granddaughter like a hunter.

Ahnah only turned when her name was called.

'Granny,' she shouted.

'Little pup!'

'It's all right,' replied Ahnah, delighted. 'This is my grandmother, Sedna, come to take me home.'

She threw her arms around her grandmother's solid middle.

'I knew you'd come.'

It was such a joyful reunion that even the policemen looked happy. Mrs Cript wiped tears from her eyes. Only Mr Cript was unimpressed.

'What I'd like to know,' he muttered, 'is how you got in here in the first place.'

'I was invited,' said Ahnah's grandmother, 'but I can't stay. I've only come to take this little one home.'

She smiled at Billy, and everybody smiled back, except Mr Cript.

'Who invited you?' he sneered, and this time he spoke more loudly. 'Don't mind me,' he said, 'I don't matter. I'm not the one in charge. I just get on with what needs doing, fixing the pipes, a leaky tap. Unblocking the drains. Out in the garden, you may notice a few things I've planted, or some things in the compost bin I've had to pull up by the roots. Weeds. Sometimes I burn 'em. Sometimes I let 'em rot down. I never let 'em get a hold. What do you say to that?'

Ahnah's grandmother tipped back her head in a way that reminded Billy of Ahnah.

'What do I say to that?' she said eventually. 'I say, what is a garden?'

It was not surprising that Ahnah's grandmother didn't know what a garden was. She had never seen one. Mr Cript couldn't believe his ears.

'What's a garden?' he repeated. 'What's a *garden*?' He laughed, looking around to show the others what a fool he thought the old lady was. 'What's a garden, indeed? Well, never mind, it's too late now. You can't teach an old dog new tricks, eh, Sedna? If your name really is Sedna, that is, and this girl, who you say is your granddaughter, really is your granddaughter.'

127

He winked at Billy, who felt his stomach turn to water.

'But let's look at it another way, shall we? Suppose this old lady is at the head of a criminal gang and these two are her accomplices? Maybe her name is Sedna. Maybe it's not. It doesn't matter. First comes the boy and makes himself at home. Then comes the little girl, with nobody to look after her. Finally, along comes Sedna, or whatever you want to call her, and announces she's the little girl's granny, come to take her home, and everybody is delighted. My wife, who

has a heart of gold, makes everybody a cup of tea. These policemen are over the moon. They can hardly believe their luck. "Off you go, Ahnah, off you go!" they say to

the little girl.
"Off you go
with Granny!"
Though they
don't know
Granny's
address, or if
her name is
Sedna or the
Abominable
Snowman. Even
though the little
girl's stolen half
the museum.'

'Stolen,' said Ahnah's grandmother, 'what has been stolen?'

'That necklace, for starters!'

'But it's Ahnah's necklace! Her grandfather made it for her.'

'Where does he live?'

'With his ancestors, just as you do.'

'Come off it! Do you think we were born yesterday?' Mr Cript gaped at the others. 'We know what's going on here – at least, I do. You're not a grandmother. You're a nasty, thieving witch and if my own grandmother was alive, she'd have known what to say to you. She'd have known what to do with these two as well. They wouldn't have been able to sit down for a week!' He smacked his hands together and whistled in appreciation.

'I don't like your grandmother,' said Ahnah, clinging more tightly to hers.

'And I don't like yours. She belongs behind bars.'

'George Arthur Cript!' gasped Mrs Cript.

'That'll be enough of that, sir,' said the first policeman, stepping between Mr Cript and Ahnah's grandmother.

'Please don't make her angry,' said Ahnah, but it was too late.

'You're right,' growled her grandmother, 'I

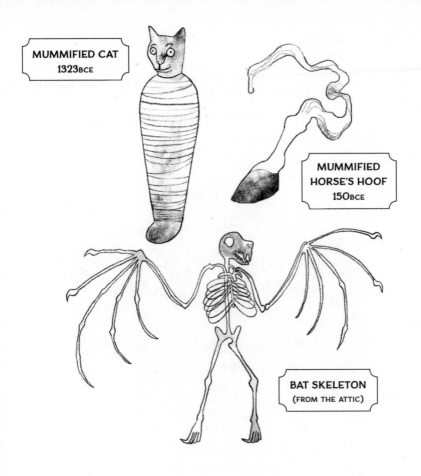

MUMMIFIED CAT
1323BCE

MUMMIFIED HORSE'S HOOF
150BCE

BAT SKELETON
(FROM THE ATTIC)

am a witch and you are a fool. It is you who is
the thief. This place is full of stolen things! But
you will never understand, and I won't waste
more time with words. You wonder if my name
really is Sedna. It is, and I will show you why.'

'Be my guest,' snarled Mr Cript.

And that was when the real trouble started.

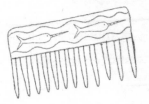

18

First, Ahnah's grandmother transformed into a polar bear. She raised her arms and pulled herself up into the huge, roaring body as if it was a hairy jumper.

'No killing, Granny, no killing,' begged Ahnah. 'Please!'

Then the bear fell onto all fours, and its legs and arms grew shorter. The hair was sucked back into its body, which changed again, becoming grey and leathery like an elephant's. The nose, which had been long and pointy, pushed in, sprouting thick white whiskers and, from the open mouth, grew the long yellow tusks of a walrus.

Finally, the stubby front legs that the walrus stood up on grew shorter still, and Sedna's body tumbled forward, dark grey and squashy. She roared again as skin closed over her mouth, and from her head, more hair began to grow. Not the pelt of a polar bear this time, but the hair of a sea witch, gushing from her

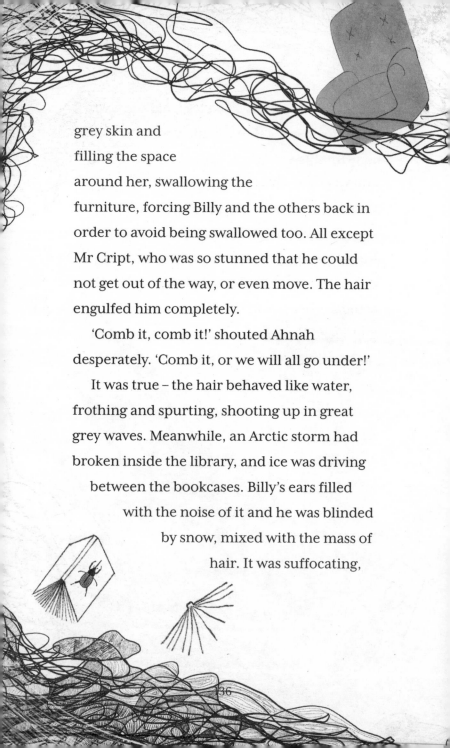

grey skin and
filling the space
around her, swallowing the
furniture, forcing Billy and the others back in
order to avoid being swallowed too. All except
Mr Cript, who was so stunned that he could
not get out of the way, or even move. The hair
engulfed him completely.

'Comb it, comb it!' shouted Ahnah
desperately. 'Comb it, or we will all go under!'

It was true – the hair behaved like water,
frothing and spurting, shooting up in great
grey waves. Meanwhile, an Arctic storm had
broken inside the library, and ice was driving
between the bookcases. Billy's ears filled
with the noise of it and he was blinded
by snow, mixed with the mass of
hair. It was suffocating,

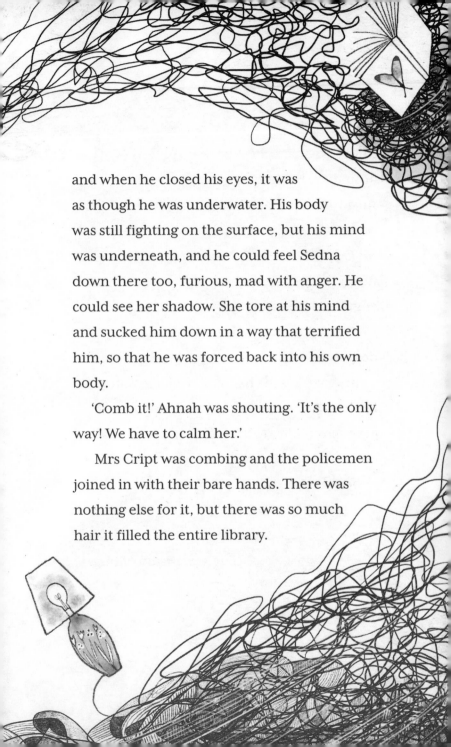

and when he closed his eyes, it was
as though he was underwater. His body
was still fighting on the surface, but his mind
was underneath, and he could feel Sedna
down there too, furious, mad with anger. He
could see her shadow. She tore at his mind
and sucked him down in a way that terrified
him, so that he was forced back into his own
body.

'Comb it!' Ahnah was shouting. 'It's the only
way! We have to calm her.'

Mrs Cript was combing and the policemen
joined in with their bare hands. There was
nothing else for it, but there was so much
hair it filled the entire library.

It surged in whirls and heaps, coiling around their arms and legs, lifting them towards the ceiling.

If only, thought Billy, *I had a proper comb.*

The idea came to him out of nowhere, as if somebody was talking to him. What he needed was a comb, and he knew which one. The comb made of narwhal horn that had been in the glass cabinet – the cabinet by the empty costume. But Billy had no way of getting upstairs to fetch it.

'Can I help?' said a sneezy, muffled sort of voice, as if somebody was trying to speak through their nose.

It was the fox, sitting on top of a floor lamp, its black eyes bright, its fur standing on end. The same fox that had come trotting into Billy's bedroom at the beginning of this story.

The fox from Ahnah's
necklace. Where had
it been all that time?
How did it know
what he needed? All
these things whizzed
through Billy's mind
in less than a second,
but his strongest
feeling was relief and
gratitude, because in
the fox's mouth was the
narwhal comb. Which may
account for its difficulty
speaking.

'Thank you,' said Billy,
taking it. He dug it into the
mass of hair, pulling with all
his strength, ripping through
the tangles. There was too
much of it.

Calm down! he
thought. *Please, calm
down. We didn't mean it. We didn't mean it. We're
sorry, we're sorry, we're sorry.*

'Give it to me!' shouted Ahnah, and seizing
the comb, she began to tear away at the hair
with both hands, and while she combed, she
sang. Billy couldn't hear the words, but it
sounded like a lullaby. He could see Mrs Cript,
with a hairbrush that must have been in her
handbag, her own hair whipping around her
face, brushing for all she was worth, and the
two policemen looking as though they were
doing the doggy paddle. It was hopeless! They
were going to die, or be buried for ever inside
the grey sea of hair. But just as Billy felt ready
to give up, Ahnah's song began to work. The

storm was still roaring, but it
wasn't as loud, and when Billy closed
his eyes, he could feel Sedna's anger
turning into something else.

Ahnah's song was like a nonsense song
you'd sing to a baby, and as she combed,
the storm disappeared altogether. The hair
untangled and was sucked back into the dark
green body of the witch, until all that was
left of Sedna's anger was the body of an old
woman, curled up like a child, sobbing.

Nearby, Mr Cript lay like a washed-up piece
of driftwood, with an expression on his face
that is hard to describe. He looked as though
everything he thought he knew had been
blasted from his brain by the things he'd seen
in Sedna's hair. It was several days before he
could utter a word.

'Oh, Granny,' said Ahnah, putting her arms around her. 'Are you all right?'

Sedna wiped her eyes and looked around her.

'Yes, I'm fine, little pup. Don't fuss.'

'Well,' said Mrs Cript. 'I think we could all do with a nice cup of tea.'

19

The policemen were the first to leave. They drank their tea and drove back to the station in silence, without switching on the siren of their police car. It was a thoughtful silence. They had been through such a lot together! When the sunburned policeman got home to his girlfriend (who was, if you remember, a geography teacher), he hugged her tightly.

Back at the house, Mrs Cript led Mr Cript upstairs by the hand, leaving the tea things to be cleared away in the morning. Mr Cript did not mind being led, because Mr Cript was not the same man. From that moment on,

he often
hesitated
before pulling
up a weed or
lighting a bonfire, in
case something might be
hiding inside it – a hedgehog,
for example, or a dormouse – and
whenever he ate in company, he was
always the last to help himself.

What had Sedna shown him though?
What horrors? In the old stories told to Inuit
children, Sedna the sea witch keeps all the
creatures of the ocean in her hair, including
the monsters, and the memories of awful
things people have done to one another. When
something goes wrong, a brave person must
go and talk to her, beneath the waves on the
seabed, and find out how to put it right. When
she is furious, her hair grows long and all
those terrible things inside it come to life, like

dark green nightmares. Her hair needs to be combed with a magical comb. It's the only way to calm her. But she can't do it herself because she has no fingers.

When the Cripts had gone to bed, Sedna sat with her granddaughter and Billy. She was perfectly calm now and her long white hair rippled quietly over her shoulders. Ahnah sat at her feet, and Billy sat opposite, with the white fox nestling on the back of his red velvet armchair.

'He likes you,' said Ahnah.

'I like him too,' said Billy, but when he tried to stroke the fox's fur, his hand passed through.

'Why does he like me?'

'Because you're a shaman.'

'But I'm not,' said Billy irritably. 'That's just my name. It doesn't mean anything. If I was called Billy Carpenter, it wouldn't make me a carpenter, would it?'

'But one of your ancestors would have been a carpenter, otherwise the name would not have been given. And one of your ancestors was a shaman. Do either of your parents have the gift?'

'I don't think so.'

Billy thought of his mum, who would be halfway up her mountain, and his dad in the rainforest, looking for something to put in a specimen box.

'Definitely not.'

'Well, no matter,' said Sedna. 'I am a shaman, but my mother was an ordinary woman. My husband was a shaman, but we did not hand down the gift to our children, though they were good hunters. Ahnah may have it; time will tell. But you have it, Billy. You have it very strongly, and this is only your first adventure. There will be many others. You heard the sleeping giant. Now he is waking up.'

'Charles said it might be bats,' said Billy hopefully.

'Perhaps it is bats,' said Sedna, smiling. 'Or perhaps it's the stars trying to talk to you, but whatever it is, you can't ignore it. It is why you are here. It is why the fox came to you. You are a shaman and you have a job to do, here in this house full of stolen things.' She shivered.

'This is a terrible place – do you feel it? Full of things that want to return home. Bodies without spirits, spirits without bodies. Dreadful.'

'It's not my fault!' said Billy. 'It wasn't me who stole them. What am I supposed to do about it?'

'Take them back.'

'All of them?' Billy thought about the huge house and everything in it, the fossils, the meteorites, the fragile skeletons of extinct mammals. Where had it all come from? When? There were too many things. It was impossible.

'I can't.'

'You can try and I believe you will succeed, because the whole world is on your side. Not only the plants and animals, but all of it, even the rocks. The stars are alive, Billy, like the fishes in the sea, and they want you to succeed. They will teach you what you need to know.

All you have to do is ask. Open your heart, as you opened your heart to me, and you will find an answer.'

'Will you help me?'

'Of course; haven't I already? But now, it's time for us to go.'

'Now?'

'Yes, it's time. Come on, little pup, where is your jacket?'

'Oh!' gasped Ahnah. 'I left it by the stream.'

'Then you will be very cold.'

'No, you won't,' said Billy, and running upstairs he came back a moment later with the jacket from the Inuit Collection.

'Here you are, but I wish you wouldn't go.'

'Can't we stay just a little while, Granny?' asked Ahnah.

'Not a moment longer,' said Sedna. 'Don't be frightened, Billy. We won't be far away, and if you ever want to visit us, light a fire as I am doing, and I will invite you in.'

She took a bowl from her pocket and,
pouring oil from a flask, blew on it as if she
was cooling soup. It burned with a blue flame
that was nearly invisible.

'Keep your heart open,' she said, 'that is my
advice to you.'

She grinned. Her teeth were yellow, like
Ahnah's necklace, with some black ones in
between.

'Goodbye,' she said.

'Goodbye,' said Ahnah, struggling into the jacket. It was much too big for her. 'You can keep mine.'

She looked at him and smiled. 'I will name one of my dogs after you.'

Then they were gone, stepping over the fire, leaving Billy alone with the books.

'I am a shaman,' he said out loud. 'I am a shaman.' He had to say it over and over again, because he didn't believe it, or was only just starting to believe. A couple of days ago, he had been Billy S, just one of three Billys in his class. Now he was Billy Shaman and the Shaman really meant something, though he was still not sure exactly what. Could he really take the shape of animals? Speak to spirits? Travel in time? If he asked Sedna to return, right now, and answer his questions, would she come? Would Ahnah? Was he really meant to return every single thing in the museum?

Every fossil? Every glass jar in the basement? And who would help him? He turned to the fox on the back of his chair, but it had gone too. He was alone in the library, which now felt large and empty. He was excited, but he was also lonely and very, very tired.

So he went to bed.

20

As for me, I slept much better that night than the night before. I dreamed of my family again, and then I dreamed of Charles. He was walking towards me, down the garden path with his hands in his pockets, as he used to. He wasn't old Charles, with the beard and the curling eyebrows. He was young Charles, with dark hair, always looking at the ground for something interesting, strolling through the mounded shells of my family until I woke up and realised that the shells were in fact cabbages and Charles was in fact Billy.

'Hello, tortoise,' he said.

'Hello, boy,' I replied.

This time he didn't pound on my shell, or kick me, or start screaming. He sat among the cabbage stalks without taking his hands out of his pockets and told me what had happened. The police. Sedna. The job he had to do. I listened and did not interrupt, or wonder if he was mad, or hiding something. Instead, I decided that I would help where I could, and when I could not give advice, I would listen and remember and eventually, when the time was right, put it all together in a story, which is what this is. At least, the beginning of a story. And I am the one telling it because nobody knows it better than me.

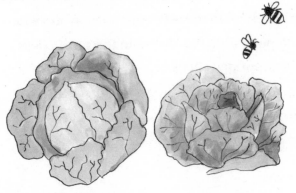

'Do you know what I like about you?' said
Billy. 'I like how you don't go anywhere. That
you sit here in the vegetable garden and when
I come to find you, you're in the same place.'

'That's all?'

'And that you're old. How old are you,
Charles?'

'Two hundred and thirty-seven.'

'Two hundred and thirty-seven years old! Impossible! It's like talking to a dinosaur.'

'Actually, I am only distantly related to a dinosaur,' I replied, but Billy wasn't listening and it was clear that there was nothing much I could tell him. I, who was born before the invention of photography, bicycles, steam trains, or even the telephone. When I was still in the egg, European explorers had not yet set foot on the North or South Pole and the hot air balloon was a novelty. But it didn't matter to Billy. I might have talked to him until I was blue in the face, but nothing would have changed, because each new creature has to discover the world in their own way, and Billy was no different.

'See you later,' he shouted, and dashing out of the garden, he set off up the stream in search of Ahnah's jacket.

It was lying where she had left it, and when Billy tried it on, he found a present in each of the pockets. In one was a half-eaten biscuit. In the other, a fox – the carved, ivory fox from Ahnah's necklace.

And here is a strange thing. Make of it what you like.

Its tail was no longer missing.

A short description
of two real people

Charles Darwin

Charles Darwin is one of the most important
scientists in history. He was also an explorer.
In 1931 he set sail aboard HMS Beagle on a
voyage around the world, collecting plants
and animals and using his pocket watch to
measure distance by measuring time.

Darwin kept a diary that became famous as
a book called *The Voyage of the Beagle*. In it, he
describes the places he visited and the strange
creatures he met, including human beings.

HMS Beagle sailed from England, across the Atlantic Ocean to South America, down the South American coast and up the other side, stopping at the Galápagos Islands before returning home by the Pacific Ocean, Australia and Africa.

Darwin returned home to England with an enormous collection of specimens: some kept in jars filled with clear alcohol, some pinned to cork, others alive, such as several young giant tortoises from the Galápagos Islands. He noticed that on each of the islands he visited, the tortoises had slightly different shells.

Darwin's second book was called *On the Origin of Species* and is even more famous than his first. It is perhaps the most important scientific book ever published. Darwin showed that all life on Earth shares a common ancestry, and that the differences between one kind of life and another occur as they adapt to the places in which they live. That's why the tortoises of the Galápagos Islands have different shells. That's why human beings are different from monkeys. But if we go far enough back in time, human beings, monkeys, tortoises, and even the ingredients of a lettuce and tomato sandwich, share the same beginning.

On the Origin of Species changed the world. It was no longer possible to claim, without going against science, that God had created human beings in his image, or that humans were more important than any other animal. Darwin continued to believe in God, but on Sundays, when his family were in church, he would go for a walk.

The house Darwin lived in for most of his life is in Kent, England, and is not quite the same as the house I have invented for my story. But it is open to the public and you can visit it. You can walk along the path Darwin called his 'Thinking Path' and admire his garden, including his vegetable patch.

The last of the tortoises that Darwin brought home from the Galápagos Islands was called Harriet and died at the age of 175, though giant tortoises can live longer. Nobody (apart from Billy) has actually met a relative of Harriet's still living among Charles Darwin's cabbages, but that does not mean there isn't one. Just because you have not met a thing does not mean it doesn't exist. Every good explorer and scientist knows that.

Pytheas

Pytheas was a real explorer. Thousands of years before Europeans set foot on the North and South Poles he discovered Thule, which was the name he gave to the 'utter north'.

Pytheas was a Greek who lived in what we now call France, in Marseilles, which was then known as Massalia. In 325 BCE he set sail from France, voyaging around the coast of England, Ireland and Scotland and up into the Arctic Circle.

Nobody knows exactly where Pytheas's journey took him, so 'Thule' became an imaginary place of ice and snow. The book Pytheas wrote about his journey was lost, but many of the things he had talked about were remembered and are not imaginary.

Pytheas was the first person on record to suggest that the moon is responsible for tides. He also noticed that, as he travelled further north, the stars changed position. He described the behaviour of Arctic ice and the midnight sun that shone without setting during the summer solstice.

Not everyone who lived at the same time as Pytheas believed that the things he had said he had seen were true. They called him a liar. But Pytheas really did make his journey, and the land he discovered was real, even though we don't know exactly where it is, or what kind of people lived there. I have written my story in a way that fills in some of the gaps.

Join Billy on
his next adventure in

Billy's second adventure takes him back to the second century BCE, when Emperor Wudi of China sent an army west to capture horses for his cavalry. The Blood Sweating Horses of Feghara were the fastest, strongest, most beautiful horses in the world. Emperor Wudi named them Heavenly Horses because he had seen them in a dream.

Now Billy is called by the best of these horses to serve its rider, Han, who is about Billy's age. It was Han's father, The Great Traveller, who discovered the horses for Wudi in the first place. Billy must help Han choose the right side, when neither the Emperor nor his rival, the Horse King, understand any language but war.

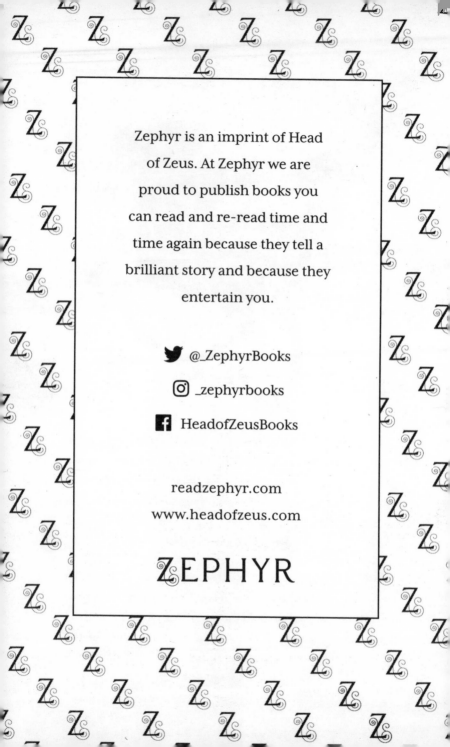

Zephyr is an imprint of Head of Zeus. At Zephyr we are proud to publish books you can read and re-read time and time again because they tell a brilliant story and because they entertain you.

🐦 @_ZephyrBooks

📷 _zephyrbooks

📘 HeadofZeusBooks

readzephyr.com

www.headofzeus.com

ZEPHYR